Bear's Christmas Star

MIREILLE D'ALLANCÉ

Bear's Christmas Star

SCHOLASTIC INC.
New York Toronto London Auckland Sydney
Mexico City New Delhi Hong Kong Buenos Aires

Bear was playing in the snow.
Papa came home with a large fir tree.

"I know what you're going to do," said Bear. "I want to help!"

Bear opened a box of garlands.
"Be careful," said Papa. "Not so fast!"

Bear tried to hang a garland all by himself.
But he couldn't reach.

"You're too small," said Papa.
"Why don't you get the rest of the decorations?"

"That's no fun," muttered Bear. "What's in here?"

"Great! Candles and . . ."
"Where's that garland?" asked Papa.

Bear held on tight to the garland.
"Let go," said Papa. "You're too small to hang it on the tree."

Aha!
Bear had an idea.

"What are you doing?" asked Papa.
"Nothing . . . nothing," said Bear.

Oh, no!
When Bear tried to attach a candle to a branch—
SMASH!
a Christmas ball fell.

"That's enough," said Papa.
"You're too small.
Get down right now . . .

and go sit over there.

Not there! Not on the Christmas balls!"

Bear ran out of the room.
The kitchen smelled like chocolate, but Bear didn't stop.

"It's not fair," whispered Bear, sitting on his bed.

Suddenly, the door opened.
"I have a problem and I need your help," said Papa.

"I don't believe you," said Bear.
"Really, I do," said Papa. "Come see."

"I'm not tall enough to put the star on top of the tree.
And if I climb on the stool . . ."
"*CRACK* goes the stool," said Bear.
"Exactly! So I need your help."

Bear grabbed the star. "You'll let me do it, Papa?"
"Promise," Papa said.
"For real?"
"For real!"

"Lie down, Papa!" said Bear.
"Like this?" asked Papa.
"No, lower!" said Bear.

HOP!
Bear leaped onto Papa's neck.

"Are we ready?" asked Papa.
"Let's go!" said Bear.

Papa stood up, holding Bear on his head.
Bear put the star on top of the Christmas tree.

"There," said Bear. "I did it!"
"Yes, you did!" said Papa.
"Do you see how it shines?" asked Bear.
"Merry Christmas, Bear."

Thank you to Béatrice, Élisabeth, and Jacques

ISBN 0-439-30974-3

Copyright © 1997 L'école des loisirs, Paris. Original title: *Couché Papa!*
English translation copyright © 2000 by Margaret K. McElderry Books.
All rights reserved.
Published by Scholastic Inc., 555 Broadway, New York, NY 10012 by arrangementwith Margaret K. McElderry Books,
an imprint of Simon & Schuster Children's Publishing Division.
SCHOLASTIC and associated logos are trademarks and/or registered trademarks of Scholastic Inc.

12 11 10 9 8 7 6 5 4 3 2 1   1 2 3 4 5 6/0

Printed in the U.S.A.   14

First Scholastic printing, November 2001